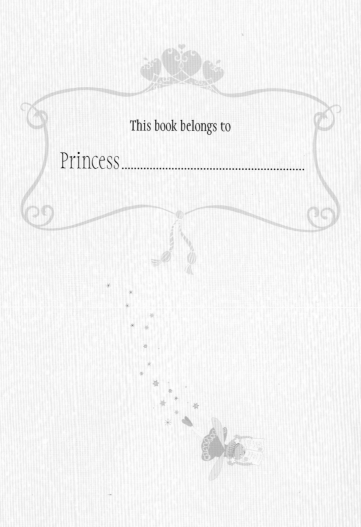

This book belongs to

Princess ....

Indian story advisor: Arisha Sattar
Photographic manipulation: John Russell
Additional illustrations by Nilesh Mistry

Picture acknowledgements

The publishers are grateful to the following for permission to reproduce material:
pages 6-7 © Archivo Iconografico, S.A./CORBIS; **page 9** © Getty Images Entertainment;
page 11 © Tim Graham; **page 13** © Ludovic Maisant/CORBIS; **page 15** © Tim Graham; **page 17** © Tim Graham;
page 19 © Stefan Lindblom/CORBIS; **page 21** © Getty Images Entertainment; **page 22** © Odd
Andersen/Pool/Reuters/Corbis; **page 23** (top) © Tim Graham/CORBIS, (bottom) © Getty Images Entertainment;
pages 36-37 © Quadrillion/CORBIS; **page 38** © Bettmann/CORBIS; **page 38-39** © Copyright The British
Museum; **page 39** (top) © Fine Art Photographic Library/CORBIS, (bottom) © Ali Meyer/CORBIS;
page 40 (top) © Rykoff Collection/CORBIS, (bottom) © Bettmann/CORBIS; **page 41** (top) © Bettmann/CORBIS,
(bottom) © Bettmann/CORBIS; **page 42** (top) © Bettmann/CORBIS, (bottom) © Getty Images Entertainment;
page 43 (top) © Wally McNamee/CORBIS, (bottom) © Tim Graham/CORBIS; **page 44** (top) © Getty Images
Entertainment, (bottom) © NOGUES ALAIN/CORBIS SYGMA; **page 45** (top) © COLLECTION PRIVEE/CORBIS
SYGMA, (bottom) © Hulton-Deutsch Collection/CORBIS; **page 46** (top) © Stephane Cardinale/CORBIS,
(bottom) © Stefan Lindblom/CORBIS; **page 47** (top) © Princess Beatrice von Preussen, (bottom left)
© Getty Images Entertainment, (bottom right) © Hans Eiberg; **page 48** © Bryan F. Peterson/CORBIS.
With thanks to Pronuptia for images of their materials and Holts
for their gemstone images (www.rholt.co.uk)

www.usborne.com
This edition first published in 2006 by Usborne Publishing Ltd.,
Usborne House, 83-85 Saffron Hill, London EC1N 8RT, England. Copyright © 2006, 2005 Usborne Publishing Ltd.

The Usborne
Little
Princess
Treasury

Susanna Davidson and Katie Daynes

Illustrated by
Maria Cristina Lo Cascio
and Shelagh McNicholas

Designed by Doriana Berkovic
Edited by Lesley Sims

With thanks to Princess Beatrice von Preussen
for her royal advice

Contents

Being a princess

Princess things for you to make

Princess scrapbook

Princess stories

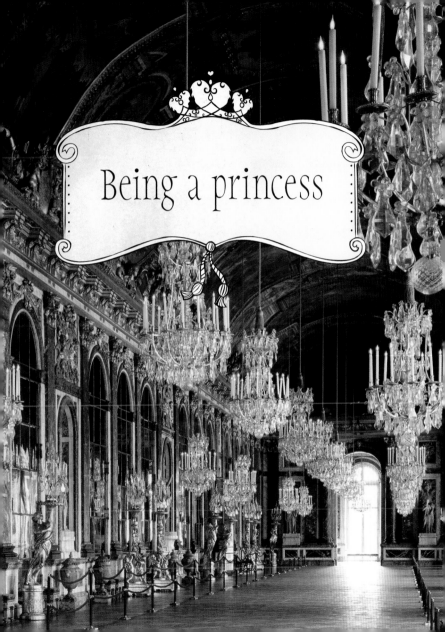

Being a princess

A princess is born

When a princess is born, everyone celebrates. People hang flags and banners from street windows, bells are rung and beacons are lit across the land. In some countries, lantern festivals are held outside the royal palace and tens of thousands of people line up to sign a book of congratulations.

Soon after the birth, the royal family gathers together for the princess's naming ceremony, or blessing. Princesses are given a string of names, sometimes as many as six or seven. A princess is usually named after her royal ancestors, and traditionally her names are chosen by the head of the royal family.

The Japanese scholars dress in traditional robes.

Different countries have their own style of naming ceremonies. In Japan, the baby princess is first washed in a cedar tub behind a white curtain. Meanwhile, scholars pluck at bow strings to ward off evil spirits and read passages from the *Chronicles of Japan*.

In Europe, baby princesses are dressed in handmade lace gowns, often lined with satin and trimmed with silk. The baby is held over a font, while an archbishop or minister sprinkles her with holy water.

This baby is Crown Princess Catharina-Amalia, future Queen of The Netherlands.

The princess's birthday may become an official flag day, when the national flag is flown from palaces and government buildings. In Thailand, the princess's birthday has even been declared a public holiday. Dance, music and arts festivals are held all over Thailand and well-wishers give money to charity.

9

Dressing up

If you shut your eyes and think of a princess dress, what do you see? A long flowing gown with a fur-lined cloak... a shining silk robe with floaty sleeves... or a sparkly dress encrusted with jewels? Throughout history, princesses around the world have worn incredible dresses, in an amazing variety of styles.

No two princesses ever dress the same.

This is how a French princess would have dressed, 500 years ago.

200 years ago, a Japanese princess would have looked like this.

An Indian princess from 100 years ago

A European princess today, dressed for a royal ball

But one thing is true for all princesses. Their clothes are always made from the very finest materials – rich velvet, delicate lace, thick furs and the softest silks. And no princess outfit is complete without jewels...

A princess's collection of jewels often begins simply, with corals and pearls given to her by royal relatives. As a princess grows up, she is given more and more splendid jewels – gifts from presidents, prime ministers and foreign royal families.

To mark a grand occasion, such as an official visit or a royal party, a princess may wear a tiara. Traditionally, princesses are given tiaras as a wedding present, either from their father or husband. The tiaras are then handed down through the family, from one generation of royals to the next.

Each stone in a tiara has a different meaning. Diamonds mean "forever" and turquoise means "true love" while amethysts represent devotion.

Princess Madeleine of Sweden wears dazzling diamonds to a royal wedding.

The Ruby Star Tiara belongs to the German royal family. The rubies represent passion.

This is the Russian Fringe Tiara, given to Princess Alexandra of Russia on her wedding day.

The Tavistock Tiara's combination of diamonds and amethysts represent eternal devotion.

The Rosse Tiara belongs to an aristocratic Irish family. It is made up of emeralds and diamonds.

The Motilla Sapphire Tiara belongs to the Spanish royal family. It can also be worn as a necklace.

Living in style

Long ago, royal families lived in constant danger. Ambitious lords or rival kings might attack at any time. So they built themselves strong, stone castles for protection, perched on rocky hilltops or surrounded by water.

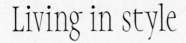

As life became more peaceful, royal families decided to move closer to their people, where it was easier to rule. Kings and queens employed the best craftsmen to make wonderful palaces. They built majestic homes in the city and magical hideaways in the countryside.

Some palaces have over 600 rooms!

Today, most princesses have two or three family homes. They might spend the winter in a remote castle with roaring fires, the summer in a beautiful waterside palace and the rest of the year in a city mansion. They may even own a royal yacht for exciting trips abroad.

Palaces have hundreds of different rooms, from a magnificent throne room with velvet curtains to a tiny washroom on the maids' corridor. A curved marble staircase leads from the main entrance to the palace's grand reception rooms, where official banquets and balls take place.

Princesses know their palaces better than anyone. They take short-cuts down the servants' stairs, hide in the butler's pantry and spy on guests from secret window seats. When no one else is around, a princess can skip across the polished ballroom floor and spin under the sparkling crystal chandeliers.

Only the royal family and servants are allowed upstairs, where the princess has her own bedroom and bathroom. She may sleep in an ornate four-poster bed... but her walls are probably plastered with posters of pop stars.

Princess lessons

For centuries, kings and queens didn't let their daughters mix with other children. Princesses were taught at home by a governess or a tutor. They learned how to be graceful, polite and charming. Other important skills included sewing, music and riding.

Embroidering patterns

Playing the harp

Riding side-saddle

Today, most princesses are sent to boarding school, where they learn normal school subjects. They also mingle with other girls – playing sports, eating meals and chatting at night in the dormitory. Only once term is over and they're back in the palace are they treated like princesses again.

Geography and current affairs are helpful subjects for a princess. It would be very embarassing to forget a prime minister's name or meet the king of a country you've never heard of.

A princess who is heir to the throne must take extra lessons. She learns the politics and law of her country, and what her official role as queen will be.

Some girls become princesses later in life, by marrying a prince. Suddenly, everyone expects them to be elegant and well-mannered. A few princess lessons are extremely useful, such as how to wave or how to greet a queen.

A princess should learn how to say "hello" in different languages.

Princess Alexandra of Denmark waves to the crowds on her way to a royal wedding.

People in the palace

The most important people in a princess's daily life are her ladies-in-waiting. These are young duchesses, ladies and countesses who give the princess support and become her closest friends. The princess also has three carefully chosen people to help organize her life.

Private secretary

Equerry

Dresser

At the beginning of each week, the princess meets with her private secretary. He's in charge of the princess's diary and knows exactly what she's doing when. It's the dresser's job to look after the princess's appearance, preparing outfits and booking haircuts. On days out, the equerry takes over. He accompanies the princess and makes sure the day runs smoothly.

Hundreds of other people
work for the royal household too.
They are ruled over by the king or queen and do
everything from stoking fires to walking the royal dogs.

Manners are extremely important in the palace. Only
close friends and family call a princess by her name.
Servants call her "Your Royal Highness" while
acquaintances call her "Ma'am" – which is
short for "madam" and rhymes with jam.

When a princess is introduced to
someone new, she smiles sweetly
and shakes their hand. If it's
someone she knows well, she
kisses them on the cheek.
But when she greets someone
more important than her,
she curtsies gracefully.

Princess Elena of
Spain curtsies to
the British Queen.

A royal banquet

A princess is expected to attend state occasions from the moment she learns to speak, but she will probably go to her first royal banquet when she is sixteen. Royal banquets take months to plan and are incredibly grand events.

Royal Menu

Champagne soup
Roast venison from the Royal Forests with wild mushrooms and rissolé potatoes
Pyramid of puff pastry
Crème brulée
Cointreau and coffee
Chocolate medallions

Guests gasp in wonder as they enter the banquet room. The table is covered in gold or silver cutlery and gold-rimmed plates. Each place has crystal glasses, which glitter in the light of the candelabras. Name labels in swirly writing show the guests where to sit – though no one may sit down before the queen. Every princess knows which cutlery to use for each course. She starts with the outermost cutlery first, then works her way in.

Side plate

Salad fork

Main course fork

Dessert fork

Napkins are expertly folded into artistic shapes.

Bread knife

Dessert spoon

Main course knife

Salad knife

Soup spoon

A princess needs to keep the conversation flowing. She looks to see if the queen talks first to the man on her left or her right, and then follows suit. She asks people about their families or their travels and never talks about herself, unless prompted.

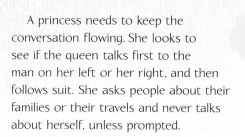
At a banquet, a princess always tries to make sure everyone is enjoying themselves.

A good princess will have read the papers that morning, so she can sound knowledgable about current affairs. Between courses she keeps her hands on her lap and *never* puts her elbows on the table.

Banquets in different countries require extra work, as a princess must learn the local customs. In Japan, she sips soup straight from her bowl. In India, she eats with her right hand only and in China, she uses chopsticks.

Princess Mary dines with other members of the Danish royal family at the Christiansborg Palace.

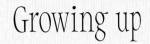

Growing up

To mark a princess's entrance into the adult world, she may attend a grand "coming-out" ball. In the past, princesses and other young ladies dressed in long white dresses and pearl necklaces. They even curtsied to a cake, which was meant to represent royalty. Today, princesses attend balls dressed in the very latest fashions and dance till dawn.

The top two layers are f[a]ke cake. The rest is made papier mâché!

As a princess grows up, she takes on more and more royal responsibilities. She makes public appearances, opening galleries and visiting schools. Some royal duties are amazingly glamorous. Princesses are asked to attend film premieres or fashion shows and even launch ships.

A vital part of a princess's role is her charity work. A princess chooses charities that are important to her, and helps to support them in every way she can. This can mean going to charity balls, helping with fundraising or visiting hospitals and talking to patients.

When a princess travels, she takes her personal staff with her. They tell her about the customs of the country, let her know who she's meeting and make sure she always has the right clothes to wear.

Trips can last months at a time and involve meeting thousands of people, including foreign royal families, presidents and prime ministers. Local people line up to see the princess and often dress in traditional costumes and put on shows.

Princess Mary of Denmark poses with young Thai dancers, on a visit to Thailand.

Getting married

In the past, a princess didn't choose her husband. Her parents arranged the marriage with another important family, sometimes before the princess was even born. Nowadays, a princess can marry for love, but her parents still want the bridegroom to be a suitable match.

Once the princess's engagement is announced, preparations begin for the big day. Thousands of people are invited to the ceremony and millions more watch it on television. Some countries set up huge screens, so excited crowds can gather to watch the wedding.

Finally it's the moment everyone's been waiting for... the arrival of the bride. Traditionally, European dresses are white (to symbolize purity), with a very long train. The princess bride may also wear the family tiara, just as her mother and grandmother did before her.

Prince Felipe of Spain with his bride, Princess Letizia

The princess's tiara must be willing to serve her country.

Younger princesses take part in weddings too. Often, they're asked to be bridesmaids. They wear pretty dresses, carry flowers, straighten the bride's train and pose for the official wedding photographs.

The British princesses Eugenie and Beatrice as bridesmaids, aged three and four

After a grand ceremony, the princess bride and her new husband parade through the streets. They wave and smile at the cheering crowds, before heading to a lavish reception at the palace.

The Crown Prince of Brunei leads his bride to their wedding banquet.

The princess changes into a stunning new outfit for the reception. She sits at the top table beside her husband and a fabulous wedding feast begins. Guests include royal families, politicians and celebrities from around the world. They shower the royal couple with generous gifts, as a symbol of friendship between their countries.

Princess things
for you to make

Design a princess door sign

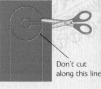

Don't cut
along this line

1. Lay a small plate or bowl near the top of a long piece of thin cardboard. Then, draw around the plate or bowl with a pencil.

2. Draw two lines from the circle to the bottom of the cardboard. Lay a small jar lid in the middle of the circle and draw around it.

3. Draw two lines from the small circle to the edge of the larger circle. Then, cut out the door sign shape, along the pencil lines.

You could give your princess a fancy nightdress, like this one.

Overlap the pillows as you glue them on.

4. Cut three large pillows from wrapping paper or an old magazine. Then, glue them across the sign, below the round hole.

If the hair is wider than the sign, trim off the edges.

5. Draw a big hairstyle on some magazine paper with hair texture on it and cut it out. Then, glue the hair across the pillows.

Glue the face over the neck and shoulders.

6. Draw a face, neck and shoulders on some paper. Cut them out and glue them to the hair, like this. Then, add a crown, too.

Trim the edges of the blanket to fit the sign.

7. For a blanket, cut a large piece of paper and glue it below the princess. Rip a strip of paper and glue it on top, then trim the edges.

8. Cut out two arms and sleeves and glue them on, like this. Glue on a flower, too. Then, write a message on the top of the sign.

Princess Rose's room

Style your own princess sash

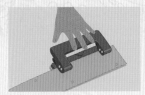

1. Cut a band of thin cardboard long enough to fit around your waist. Then, use a hole puncher to make holes along the long edges.

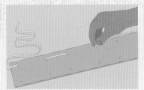

2. Cut two pieces of ribbon, twice as long as the sash. Thread one ribbon in and out of the holes along the top of the sash, like this.

Pull the ribbons so they dangle from both ends of the sash.

3. Thread the other ribbon through the holes along the bottom. Then, tape the ribbons at both ends of the sash.

4. Draw lots of flowers, circles and tiny hearts on some different patterned wrapping papers. Then, cut them out.

5. Turn the sash over, so the tape is on the back. Then, glue the flowers, circles and hearts on the sash to decorate it.

6. To make the rosette, cut out a large flower from wrapping paper. Curl the edges of the petals by rolli each one around a pencil.

7. Cut two slightly smaller flowers, from different patterned papers. Make one smaller than the other. Curl their petals, too.

8. Glue the three flowers on top of each other in order of size, like this. Use a ballpoint pen to make two holes in the middle.

9. Thread a pipe cleaner through one of the holes. Turn the rosette over, ben the pipe cleaner and threa it through the other hole.

28

You can decorate your sash and rosette with sequins, beads and stickers, too.

10. Twist the ends of the pipe cleaner into spirals. Then, cut out a large leaf and tape it to the back of the rosette.

11. Glue the rosette near one end of the sash and leave the glue to dry. Then, tie the sash around your waist with the rosette to one side.

Create a sparkly tiara

Only cut halfway into the band.

1. Cut a narrow band of thin cardboard that fits once around your head. Then, cut a little off one of the ends.

2. A little way from one end, make a cut going down into the band. Then, make a second cut going up into the other end.

3. Cut seven strips of foil that are twice as wide as the band. Then, squeeze and roll them to make thin sticks.

You could use shiny cardboard for the band.

You can bend the foil sticks in different ways to make all kinds of tiaras.

Try hanging a
paper heart from
a piece of thread.

The tiara sits on the top
of your head. You may need
to clip it to your hair.

Leave some
space at each
end of the band.

. Cut each stick in half.
hen, bend one piece in
alf so that it makes an
rch. Tape it onto the
iddle of the band.

5. Bend the rest of the
foil sticks and tape three
arches on either side of
the middle one. Then,
turn the tiara over.

6. Decorate the front of
the tiara with stickers and
sequins. Then, slot its
ends together so that the
ends are inside, like this.

Make a swish princess bag

You don't need this part, but you will need the handles.

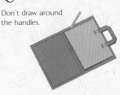
Don't draw around the handles.

1. Flatten a paper sandwich bag and use a ruler to draw a line across it. Cut along the line, through all the layers of the bag.

2. Cut the handles off the top of the bag. Paint them, and the sides of the bag, red. When the paint is dry, tape the handles on.

3. Lay the bag on a piece of thin red cardboard. Draw around it twice and cut out both rectangles. Glue one to the back of the bag.

The lid of a spice jar is a good size.

4. Draw around the lid of a small jar to make lots of circles on pieces of red, pink and gold cardboard or thick paper. Then, cut them out.

The circles on your bag will swish as you carry it.

You could make a little purse like this to match your bag.

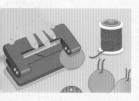

5. Use a hole puncher to make a hole near the edge of each circle. Then, push a short thread through the hole in each circle.

6. With the thread at the top, lay one circle in the bottom corner of the spare red rectangle. Tape the thread in place.

The number of circles you need will depend on the size of your bag.

7. Tape more circles all along the bottom of the rectangle, in the same way. They should overlap each other slightly at the sides.

You can decorate your bag with hearts or a bow, too.

8. Tape another row of circles above the first row, so each circle hangs over the one below it. Add more rows to fill the rectangle.

9. Then, glue the decorated rectangle to the front of the bag. For a fur trim, glue cotton balls and sequins along the top of the bag.

A princess fan for a ball

The crayon lines are shown here in yellow so that you can see them.

1. Using a white crayon, draw lots of swirly lines on a large piece of white paper. Fill the paper with the shapes.

2. Then, cover the paper with pale, watery paint. While it is wet, paint a wide band of a different shade across the middle.

3. Paint two narrower da▮ stripes along the top and bottom of the paper. The darker stripes will blur into the pale background▮

You could decorate your fan with gold or silver pen.

Be careful not to cut all the way across.

4. When it is dry, fold the left-hand edge of the paper in by the width of two fingers. Turn the paper over and do the same again.

5. Keep folding and turnin▮ until the paper is folded. Cut a tiny triangle out of each end. Then, cut triangles along one edge.

Fold the fan in half and unfold it again. Glue half of the fan. Then, fold the fan again, pressing the two sides firmly together.

Cut the strip the same width as the fan.

7. For a handle, cut a strip of cardboard that is over twice the height of the fan. Fold the strip in half, then unfold it again.

8. Glue the folded fan to one end of the strip. Spread glue over the rest of the strip and fold it in half to meet the top of the fan.

Squeeze the two sides of the folded strip together firmly to make a handle below the fan. Then, open out the fan.

You can cut different shaped holes in your fans to make pretty patterns.

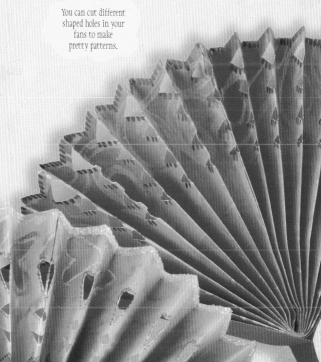

Princess scrapbook

Princesses of the past

Captivating Cleopatra

Over two thousand years ago, there lived a beautiful princess named Cleopatra. Daughter of Pharaoh Ptolemy of Egypt, she grew up in a magnificent palace by the sea. Cleopatra loved reading and could speak Egyptian, Latin and Greek. When Cleopatra's father died, scheming Greeks took over the country. Cleopatra turned to the Roman leader, Julius Caesar, for help. Captivated by the intelligent princess, Caesar used his power to make her Egypt's queen.

Egyptian princesses wore lots of gold and sparkling jewels.

Immortal fame

Cleopatra's story has enchanted people for hundreds of years. In the 16th century, Shakespeare wrote a play about her. She has been the subject of many ballets and, in 1962, a Hollywood film starring Elizabeth Taylor was made about her life.

This stone carving of Cleopatra is thousands of years old.

The Tudor princesses

Mary and Elizabeth Tudor had different mothers, but the same father – King Henry VIII of England. Henry was so desperate for a son, he kept changing wives until he got one. He also rejected Mary and Elizabeth and took away their title of princess. The sisters were rivals and never got along. When Mary became queen, she locked Elizabeth in a tower so she didn't cause trouble. Five years later, Mary died and Elizabeth took over the throne.

Queen Elizabeth I

"Do so much good to the French that they can say I sent them an angel."

The Empress of Austria to her daughter, Marie Antoinette

Marie Antoinette

Marie Antoinette was the fifteenth child of the Empress of Austria. She had a happy, carefree childhood, riding through the royal forests, playing her harp, embroidering and dancing. But at twelve years old, she discovered she was to marry the future king of France. She had to learn French quickly, study the history of France and wear braces to straighten her teeth.

Marie Antoinette

39

Russian royalty

Anastasia was born in 1901. She was the daughter of Tsar Nicholas II, ruler of the Russian Empire and the richest man in the world. As a young princess, she liked painting, lying in the sun and taking photos.

In 1914, the First World War broke out. Many wounded soldiers were taken to a hospital near the royal palace, where Anastasia and her sisters helped treat them and cheer them up.

A sad ending

In 1917, Anastasia's world was shattered. The people of Russia started a revolution and forced Tsar Nicholas from the throne. Anastasia and her family were imprisoned in a guarded house. They sang hymns and prayed to keep up their spirits. But one awful summer night, men stormed the building and killed the whole family.

In this family photo, Anastasia is the one on the far right.

Elizabeth and Margaret

Elizabeth is the older sister, on the left.

The English princesses Elizabeth and Margaret were like chalk and cheese – Elizabeth the quiet, sensible one and Margaret the mischievous, charming one. They never imagined their father would rule England but, in 1936, their uncle, King Edward VIII, gave up the throne to marry a divorced woman. The following year the princesses saw their father crowned King George VI at Westminster Abbey.

Heir to the throne

Aged ten, Elizabeth was suddenly heir to the throne. Her education at home was quickly altered to include British history and law. In 1939, war began and both princesses were moved to the countryside for safety. Elizabeth was fourteen when she performed her first public duty – a radio broadcast to the children of wartime Britain. Twelve years later, her father died... and she became Queen Elizabeth II.

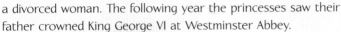

"We children at home are full of cheerfulness and courage."

Princess Elizabeth in her radio broadcast, 1940

Becoming a princess

Hollywood star

Her Serene Highness Princess Grace of Monaco started life as plain Grace Kelly. She always dreamed of becoming an actress, and by the age of twenty-two had starred in her first film. Grace went on to become one of the most famous actresses of her day. Then, in 1955, she met Prince Rainier of Monaco at the glamorous Cannes Film Festival. A year later they were married. Grace gave up her career to devote her time to being a wife, mother and princess.

Spanish flair

Letizia Ortiz was famous in Spain even before she married Crown Prince Felipe. She worked as a TV newsreader, reporting on dramatic events around the world. Then, in 2002, she met and fell in love with Felipe. For months they kept their relationship secret, so their engagement came as a complete surprise to the people of Spain. But everyone was delighted. The newspapers declared Letizia a queen for the 21st century.

Princess Diana

When Lady Diana Spencer became engaged to Prince Charles her life changed overnight. She went from being a shy kindergarten teacher to one of the most photographed women in the world. Millions of people watched their fairytale wedding on TV and the London streets were packed with onlookers.

"I'd like to be queen of people's hearts."

Princess Diana

Caring for others

Princess Diana was patron of over a hundred charities and kept working for many of them even after her marriage ended. Tragically, at the age of thirty-six, Princess Diana died in a car accident. Thousands of people flocked to Kensington Palace, where she'd lived, to lay down flowers and pay their respects.

Princesses today

Gifted scholar

Chulabhorn, the youngest daughter of the King and Queen of Thailand, is not just an important princess – she is also a highly gifted scientist. She has won prizes for her work and has even opened her own research institute. As well as being a wife and mother, she also represents her country at events around the world.

Princess Chulabhorn with her mother in 1966, when she was nine years old.

Wild rose

Princess Kalina's name means "wild rose" and as a teenager she was often rebellious. But Kalina didn't always have to behave like a princess. Her father, the King of Bulgaria, had been forced to flee his country, and Kalina grew up in Spain. In 1993, the royal family's land was returned to them just in time for Kalina to marry her husband in a beautiful palace in the Bulgarian mountains.

Princess for president

Esther Kamatari, a Burundian princess, fled to France at the age of nineteen, after her father and her uncle, the King of Burundi, were murdered. Ten years later, she was Europe's first black supermodel. Since the 1990s she has worked tirelessly to help war orphans in Burundi and in 2004 she returned to her country to run for president.

An extraordinary life

Princess Elizabeth of Toro was born in Uganda, East Africa, to the Toro royal family at the height of its glory. She excelled at school and went on to become Uganda's first woman lawyer. Then, in 1967, the Toro royal family was thrown out by the government. Elizabeth moved to the USA, where she became a successful actress and model.

But Elizabeth never forgot her country. She stayed involved in Ugandan politics, even though it put her life in danger. In 1993, the Toro royal family was restored and Elizabeth was able to return as Princess Royal to serve her people.

45

Skilled rider

Princess Haya Bint Al Hussein of Jordan is both an athlete and a dedicated charity worker. At the age of thirteen she was chosen to represent her country at show jumping. She went on to

show jump all over the world and, in 2000, was the first Arab woman to compete on horseback at the Olympic Games. She is also the first and only woman in Jordan with permission to drive a truck.

"My father's nickname for me is The Trucker."

Princess Haya

A future queen

Crown Princess Victoria of Sweden will one day become queen – the first in Sweden for over two hundred years. Traditionally, the heir to the Swedish throne had to be a boy, but in 1980 Sweden changed its laws so that Victoria could become queen. Now the eldest child, girl or boy, can inherit the throne.

Part-time princess

Beatrice von Preussen is princess
to a country that no longer exists.
Von Preussen means "of Prussia"
in German, but the Kingdom of
Prussia collapsed over eighty years
ago. So Beatrice lives a life like any other girl
in England. In Germany, however, people still treat
her family like royalty and Beatrice loves being
able to act like a proper princess when she is there.
She borrows her mother's jewels, which have been handed
down through generations of princesses, dresses up in
ball gowns and attends grand events.

This shows Princess
Beatrice when she was six
years old, with her younger
sister, Florence.

Princess Aiko

The people of Japan were delighted when Crown
Princess Aiko was born in December 2001. Thousands
lined up to sign a book of congratulations and
there were street parades and lantern festivals all
over Japan. Aiko's name, which combines the
words for *child* and *love*, was carefully
chosen by her parents. They also
chose her symbol, the white-
flowered Asian azalea, in the hope
that she will grow to have a pure
heart like the pure-white flower,

47

Princess stories

Twelve Dancing Princesses
A German fairy tale based on a story from the Brothers Grimm

The Dragon Princess
A 2000-year-old Chinese fairy tale from the Han Dynasty

The Princess and the Pea
A Danish fairy tale first written down by Hans Christian Andersen

Nala and Damayanti
A story from the Mahabharata, an Indian epic

The Frog Princess
A traditional Russian folk tale

Twelve Dancing Princesses

In a grand old castle, surrounded by royal forests, lived an old king and his many daughters. There were twelve princesses in all, each as beautiful as the next. They spent their days reading and playing music. What they wanted more than anything was to dance, but dancing was forbidden by their father.

Their mother, the queen, had been the most elegant dancer in the kingdom. When she died, the king was inconsolable. He locked up the royal ballroom, threw away the key and no one had seen him smile since. For years, the princesses begged their father to let them dance, but he always refused. Finally, they gave up... or so he thought.

One morning, the king noticed his castle was quieter than usual. It was almost noon and he hadn't seen even one of his daughters. He sent a maid to find out where they were.

"Please Your Highness," said the maid, scampering back to the king's throne. "They're still fast asleep in their beds... and I found this by their bedroom door." She handed a dainty dance shoe to the king. Its sole was dirty and worn through.

"WHAT!" cried the king, almost exploding. "Which daughter *dares* go dancing?"

"If you please, Your Highness," the maid went on, "I counted twenty-three more shoes in the pile."

"No one dances in *my* kingdom," boomed the angry king. "Especially not my daughters. Tonight, I shall lock their room."

True to his word, the king waited until the princesses had gone to bed and locked their heavy oak door. The following morning, he was pleased to see his daughters sleeping peacefully.

But then he spied a pile of shoes in the corner, their soles worn thin with dancing. "Burn those shoes!" the king ordered a servant. "And get the locksmith to add two more locks."

All day, the king was in a terrible temper. As for the princesses, they sat yawning and giggling behind their books. The next morning, and every morning for a week, the king found yet more worn-out dance shoes. Even with ten locks on the door, two guards outside and extra bolts on the windows, his daughters still managed to sneak away and go dancing.

The king was slowly going crazy with frustration.
His dreams became haunted with dancing and laughter.
"Tell me where you dance," he pleaded with his daughters.
"We don't know what you mean," was their reply.

Eventually, he made an announcement to his kingdom.
"Discover where my daughters dance at night and you may
marry whichever one you choose," he proclaimed. "But
waste my royal time and I'll imprison you in my dungeon."
Before long, an arrogant prince arrived at the castle.
"I'll solve the mystery, Your Highness," he said, confidently.
"I hope you can..." sighed the king.

The prince was shown to a room next to the princesses'
bedroom. A bed was prepared for him, but he knew better
than to sleep. That night, the princesses walked past his
room. They curtsied, blew a kiss and whispered goodnight.
The youngest even gave the prince a cup of hot chocolate.
"Soon, one of those princesses will be my wife," thought
the prince. As he waited for the sisters to creep off to dance,
he took a long sip of chocolate. "Mmmmm," he murmured,
resting his head on the pillow for just a moment...
before falling fast asleep.

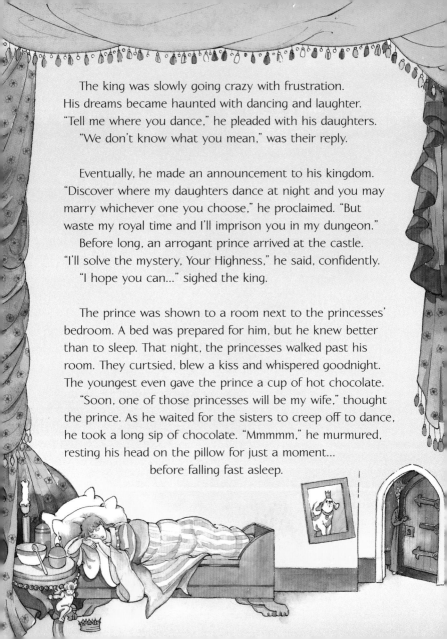

When the prince awoke, sun was already streaming through the window. He jumped up in a panic, raced into the princesses' room and tripped over a heap of dance shoes. The princesses giggled to see the prince half buried in their shoes. The king, however, was far from amused. He sent the prince straight to the dungeon and became increasingly grumpy.

In the weeks that followed, ten more hopeful princes came to the castle. One by one, they sat in the little bedroom, determined to follow the sisters. But none of them managed to stay awake. By the end of the month, they were all in the dungeon and the princesses were dancing more than ever.

Meanwhile, a handsome soldier was riding home when he heard the story of the twelve dancing princesses. He decided to try his own luck and headed for the royal castle.

"Where are you going?" asked a wizened old woman as he rode by.

"To discover how the princesses dance their shoes to pieces," he replied.

The woman thought the soldier looked honest and wise. "You'll need this," she said, handing him a cloak. "Wear it and you will become invisible. Just be careful not to drink anything the princesses offer you."

The soldier thanked the woman and rode on to the castle.

When he arrived, the king was near despair. "How can a soldier succeed where so many princes have failed?" he asked.

"I can only try my best," said the soldier.

He was shown to the small bedroom shortly before nightfall. One by one, each princess wished him goodnight and the youngest held out a cup of creamy hot chocolate.

"Thank you," said the soldier, smiling.

As the princess dashed away, the soldier poured the tempting drink into a plant pot and watched the leaves go droopy. Then he lay, fully-dressed, under the covers and waited with his eyes tightly closed.

"He's asleep," called a voice.

"Let's go," cried another.

Draping the old woman's cloak around him, the soldier crept into the princesses' bedroom. They were all dressed in exquisite ball gowns and sparkling new dance shoes.

"Ready?" asked the eldest sister, standing by her four-poster bed. She tapped the bed frame three times and immediately it slid across the floor, revealing a narrow staircase. With a flurry of bright silks and satins, the twelve princesses descended the stairs, followed by the invisible soldier. In his eagerness, he stepped on the hem of the youngest princess's dress. She looked around... saw nothing and frowned.

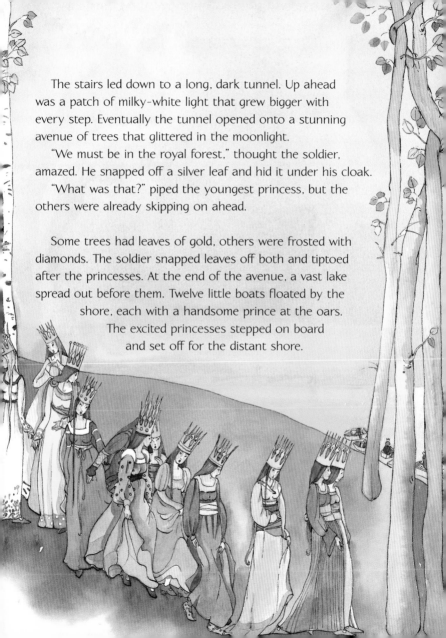

The stairs led down to a long, dark tunnel. Up ahead was a patch of milky-white light that grew bigger with every step. Eventually the tunnel opened onto a stunning avenue of trees that glittered in the moonlight.

"We must be in the royal forest," thought the soldier, amazed. He snapped off a silver leaf and hid it under his cloak.

"What was that?" piped the youngest princess, but the others were already skipping on ahead.

Some trees had leaves of gold, others were frosted with diamonds. The soldier snapped leaves off both and tiptoed after the princesses. At the end of the avenue, a vast lake spread out before them. Twelve little boats floated by the shore, each with a handsome prince at the oars. The excited princesses stepped on board and set off for the distant shore.

"Why is my boat lower in the water tonight?" wondered the youngest princess. She couldn't see the soldier perched on the bow, hugging his knees under his magic cloak.

Gradually a fairytale palace came into view. Wisps of music floated across the lake and snatches of laughter hung in the air. Moments later, the princes and princesses were dancing through the maze of a magical garden. The soldier was captivated by the scene. Still hidden by his cloak, he wove his way among the dancers, following one princess in particular – the youngest.

At the first sign of dawn, the princes and princesses
reluctantly returned to their boats. The twelve sisters retraced
their footsteps to the castle, their dainty dance shoes worn
to pieces. Ahead of them ran the invisible soldier. He was
determined to be in bed when the princesses arrived.

"He's still sleeping," whispered the eldest sister, out of breath
from climbing the narrow stairs. The happy sisters murmured
goodnight to each other and were soon fast asleep.

Before the servants had even laid the breakfast table, the triumphant soldier strolled up to the king.

"I suppose you want to know the way to the dungeon," said the king, wearily.

"No, Your Royal Highness," replied the soldier. "I would like to claim my reward."

"Reward?" cried the king. "You mean to say..."

"I know where your daughters dance," finished the soldier. He described the secret staircase, the avenue of trees, the vast lake and the fairytale palace.

The king looked unconvinced, so the soldier produced the silver, gold and diamond leaves. Still unsure, the king summoned his daughters. When they saw the leaves, they sighed and confessed everything.

"I must thank you," said the king to the soldier. "Now I can finally stop my daughters from dancing. Which one do you choose as your bride?"

"I would very much like to marry your youngest daughter," replied the soldier, "if she will agree to be my wife..."

"Oh yes!" said the youngest princess, beaming.

"Then the marriage shall take place in a week," announced the king. "I shall hold a sumptuous feast for all the kingdom."

"Thank you sir," said the soldier, bowing. "But surely a marriage would not be complete without dancing..."

The king looked very stern indeed. "Since my dear wife's death, there has been no dancing in this castle."

"But Father," pleaded the youngest princess. "Mother would have wanted us to dance and be happy."

The king quickly turned away, to hide his tears. "Very well," he said solemnly. "You may dance." He ordered his footmen to break down the ballroom door, then an army of maids dusted the furniture and polished the floor.

As the sun set on the youngest princess's wedding day, her sisters gathered in the ballroom and the royal band began to play. The soldier led his bride onto the dance floor and they glided together in an elegant waltz. When the youngest princess looked across at her father, she saw that even he was smiling.

The Dragon Princess

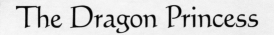

Deep deep down, at the bottom of the Eastern Sea, lived the Dragon King and his beautiful daughter. In his human form, the Dragon King dressed in rich silk robes and glittering rings. But when he was angry he became a dragon... and he was angry now. He tore along the corridors of his underwater palace and burst into the Dragon Princess's room.

"Daughter!" he bellowed, breathing fire. "What's this I hear? You've rejected yet another suitor. And this time it was the King of Ching River! You must marry *someone*!"

The Dragon Princess sighed and twirled her black hair between her fingers. "I don't want a rich or powerful man," she said sadly. "Just find me a boy who is honest and brave."

For three days, the Dragon King stomped his feet and gnashed his teeth. But he couldn't bear to see his daughter unhappy. So he called for Admiral Lobster and Marshal Crab, General Eel and Prime Minister Turtle.

"Find my daughter a brave and honest husband," he demanded.

After much searching, General Eel came before the Dragon King and his daughter. "I have found the perfect man," he said. "His name is Ayer. He's a poor man, but a good one. He lives in a village at the bend of a river."

The Dragon Princess smiled, but the Dragon King was furious. "How do we know if this man is really honest?" he fumed. "He's not even a member of our Water Tribe. I don't think it's a suitable match."

"But I do," said the Dragon Princess, storming off to her room. She stayed there for seven days and seven nights and refused to speak to anyone.

The Dragon King didn't know what to do. Luckily, Admiral Lobster had a plan. That very night, Ayer dreamed an old man, dressed in shining white, came to him and said, "Go down to the water's edge tonight. There you will see your future wife."

61

Ayer opened his eyes with a start. "What a strange vision," he thought. He woke his elder brother, Ahda, and described his dream to him.

"Sounds like nonsense to me," said Ahda grumpily. "Just go back to sleep!"

But as soon as Ayer was asleep, Ahda crept out of the hut and ran down to the water's edge. When Ayer woke again, his brother was nowhere to be seen. "He must have gone down to the river," thought Ayer. Flinging on his clothes, he ran after him.

The water lay still and silvery under the great round moon. On a rock in the middle of the river sat a beautiful girl.

"Marry me!" cried Ahda, gazing at her greedily.

"Marry *me*!" pleaded Ayer.

"Which of you is honest and brave?" asked the Dragon Princess.

"I am," answered the brothers together.

"I shall set you a test to see," said the Dragon Princess. "I'll marry the man who brings me the pearl that shines in the dark."

"How do we find it?" asked Ayer.

"You must go to the palace of my father, the mighty Dragon King of the Eastern Sea," said the princess. She plucked two combs from her hair and gave them to the brothers. "These are water-parting combs," she said. "Use them to make your way into the sea."

The two brothers bowed to the princess. Ahda rushed away from the river. He borrowed a horse and galloped east. Ayer set off on foot, following the river as it wound its way to the sea.

After many days of travel, Ahda was tired and hungry. He had nearly finished his supplies when he came to a village that had been flooded by water. Only the tops of the houses poked above the surface. The villagers sat huddled on the rooftops, staring at their ruined village.

"What happened here?" Ahda asked.

"Ten days ago a great flood came," replied a villager. "The water keeps rising all the time. We've lost our homes, our crops... We need to stop the flood."

"And only one thing can do that," added the eldest villager. "We need the magic Golden Dipper from the Dragon King's treasure chamber."

Ahda thought a moment before answering. "I'm on my way there now," he said. "Give me something to eat and I'll bring back the Golden Dipper for you."

Hungry as they were, the villagers gathered together some scraps of food and gave them to Ahda.

A few days later Ayer arrived at the same village. Seeing the flood, he offered to help. "We need the Golden Dipper from the Dragon King's palace," said the villagers.

"Then I'll get it for you," promised Ayer, and went on his way.

When at last Ayer came to the shore of the Eastern Sea, he was astonished to find his brother still there, looking in alarm at the roaring waves. Ayer bravely gripped the Dragon Princess's comb and dived into the sea. At once, the waves rolled back, rising higher and higher, until they showed the path to the palace. Nervously, Ahda followed Ayer. At the palace entrance stood the Dragon King himself.

"Welcome," he said. "I've been expecting you. Follow me to the treasure chamber."

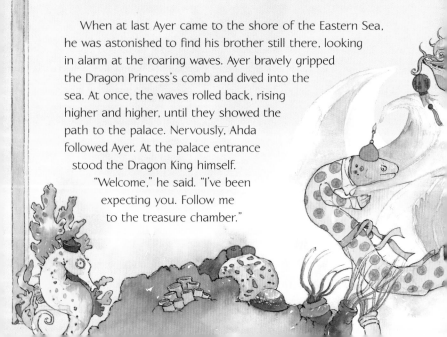

Ayer and Ahda gasped as they entered the chamber. Its sparkling walls were covered in diamonds and the floor was studded with emeralds. But the brightest light of all came from a shining pearl, resting in its shell. "Take whatever you like," said the Dragon King. "But you mustn't take more than one piece."

At this news, Ayer's heart grew heavy. He couldn't take the pearl now. Instead he looked for the Golden Dipper...
...while Ahda stuffed the shining pearl into his bag.

The two brothers left the palace together. Once they reached the shore, Ahda leaped onto his horse and sped away as fast as he could. When he came to the flooded village, the villagers crowded around him, crying, "Where is the Golden Dipper?"

"The Dragon King wouldn't give it to me," Ahda lied, and he rode off without a second glance.

When Ayer arrived, he called out to the villagers. "Look!" he cried. "I have the Golden Dipper!" With shouts of joy, the villagers slid down from their rooftops and began bailing out the water with the Dipper. With one scoop, the water rushed out of the houses. With the second, it disappeared from the fields. With the third, it vanished completely.

"How can we thank you?" asked the eldest villager. "We have nothing left to give." But then his eyes lit upon a large black oyster, lying half submerged in the mud. He picked it up and pulled it open. Inside was a huge black pearl. The eldest villager handed the pearl to Ayer. "Please accept this," he said, "as a token of our thanks."

Ayer smiled and took the pearl. "I was happy to help," he replied. But as he walked back to the village, he couldn't help thinking of the Dragon Princess.

Meanwhile, Ahda had arrived at the river bend. Proudly, he walked up to the Dragon Princess. "I have the pearl that shines in the dark," he said. "Take it, and become my wife."

"It is not yet time," replied the princess. "Come back tonight, when I will decide if you have the right pearl."

Ahda returned that night. He opened the shell and held up the pearl. But no light shone.

"It's the wrong pearl," explained the Dragon Princess.

Ahda screamed and stamped his feet. Then, before his furious gaze, the pearl disappeared, leaving a dirty drop of water in the palm of his hand.

The following night, Ayer arrived at the river's edge. Ahda followed close behind him. The Dragon Princess was waiting for them.

"I don't have your pearl," said Ayer, sadly.

"Then what are you carrying in your bundle?" asked the Dragon Princess.

"Not the pearl you want," said Ahda.

"Let me be the judge of that," said the Dragon Princess.
She held out her hand and Ayer gave her the pearl.

The next instant, Ayer had to shield his eyes. The pearl
was no longer black, but shining brighter than the moon.
The Dragon Princess flung the pearl high into the air.
It crackled and fizzed like a firework, then split into
thousands of fiery sparks.

When Ayer looked up, he saw the surface of
the river part. The shiny red rooftops of the
Dragon King's palace rose up and out of
the river until they touched the sky.
The Dragon Princess took Ayer's hand.

"This is where you belong now," she said. "You have proved you have a kind and brave young heart." And she led Ayer into the palace.

"No!" cried Ahda. He chased after them, but dragons leaped down from the rooftops and barred his way. He shouted after them, but Ayer and the Dragon Princess never looked back.

Ahda saw their clothes change into wedding robes and heard music and laughter on the wind. Then the palace sank back into the water, leaving Ahda alone in the dark.

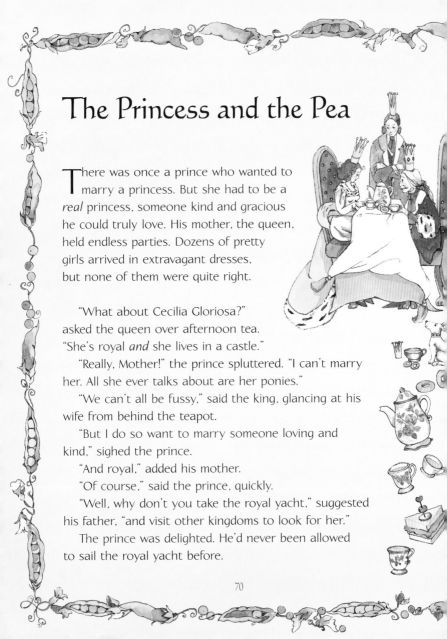

The Princess and the Pea

There was once a prince who wanted to marry a princess. But she had to be a *real* princess, someone kind and gracious he could truly love. His mother, the queen, held endless parties. Dozens of pretty girls arrived in extravagant dresses, but none of them were quite right.

"What about Cecilia Gloriosa?" asked the queen over afternoon tea. "She's royal *and* she lives in a castle."

"Really, Mother!" the prince spluttered. "I can't marry her. All she ever talks about are her ponies."

"We can't all be fussy," said the king, glancing at his wife from behind the teapot.

"But I do so want to marry someone loving and kind," sighed the prince.

"And royal," added his mother.

"Of course," said the prince, quickly.

"Well, why don't you take the royal yacht," suggested his father, "and visit other kingdoms to look for her."

The prince was delighted. He'd never been allowed to sail the royal yacht before.

70

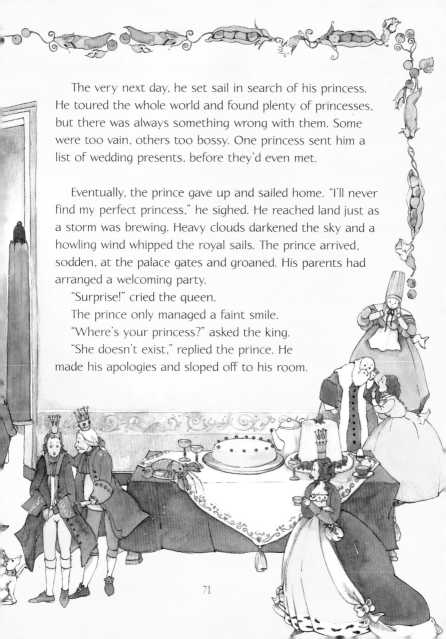

The very next day, he set sail in search of his princess. He toured the whole world and found plenty of princesses, but there was always something wrong with them. Some were too vain, others too bossy. One princess sent him a list of wedding presents, before they'd even met.

Eventually, the prince gave up and sailed home. "I'll never find my perfect princess," he sighed. He reached land just as a storm was brewing. Heavy clouds darkened the sky and a howling wind whipped the royal sails. The prince arrived, sodden, at the palace gates and groaned. His parents had arranged a welcoming party.

"Surprise!" cried the queen.

The prince only managed a faint smile.

"Where's your princess?" asked the king.

"She doesn't exist," replied the prince. He made his apologies and sloped off to his room.

That night, the prince watched the
storm outside and felt lonelier than ever.
Suddenly, in a flash of lightning, he saw
the silhouette of a small figure approaching
the castle. Moments later, there was a muffled
knocking. The curious prince crept onto the landing.
He felt a blast of wind as his father opened the heavy
oak door and gasped in wonder at the sight before him.

There, on the doorstep, stood a shivering girl.
Even soaked to the skin and splattered with dirt, she
looked absolutely beautiful. "I'm so sorry to bother
you, Your Royal Highness," she said timidly. "My coach
is stuck in the mud and my horse has broken free.
I'll never reach my Grandmother's tonight."
    "Oh," said the king. "Well come inside, Miss..."
    "Princess Margherita," said the girl, curtsying.
    "A princess?" whispered the prince, excitedly.
    "A princess?" cried the queen, appearing in her
dressing gown. "Wait there, dear, while I organize
a room for you." She sent for two maids and
            headed off down the corridor, a
                mischievous twinkle in her eye.

The prince looked on, spellbound, as the princess stood dripping in the hall. She looked up at him and smiled. Mesmerized, they just gazed at each other until, finally, a maid showed the princess to her room.

"She's perfect!" exclaimed the prince, seeing his mother.

"We'll see about that," the queen replied. "First, she'll have to pass the princess test. I've placed a pea on her bed. Then I ordered the maids to pile twenty mattresses on top. If she's a real princess, she won't sleep a wink."

"And neither shall I," sighed the prince.

Next morning, the prince was first down to breakfast. He yawned and stirred his tea until it was cold. At last, the king and queen arrived, but there was still no sign of the girl.

"She must have overslept," said the queen. "What a pity."

"No... look," said the prince, his eyes lighting up. "She's here!"

"Good morning, Margherita," the queen said, kindly. "I trust you slept well?"

"Actually..." replied Margherita, nervously.

"Go on," urged the prince.

"Don't be shy," said the king.

"To be honest, I didn't sleep at all," she said. "There must have been something lumpy in my bed. I'm covered in bruises."

"That's wonderful," said the prince. "I mean, poor you."

"Well, *Princess* Margherita," said the king, clapping his hands. "Welcome to the family."

"Father!" cried the prince, blushing crimson. "What he means is... Well, what I mean is..." The bashful prince got down on one knee. "Will you marry me?"

Princess Margherita seemed lost for words.

"I've been too hasty," thought the prince. "She doesn't even know me." But as he watched, her lips curved into a smile.

"Yes please," she whispered.

The prince was the happiest man in the kingdom.

A month later, the king and queen held a magnificent wedding for their son and his real princess. Guests arrived from all over the world. And there, on proud display on the best royal cushion, sat a bright green pea.

Nala and Damayanti

Nala, King of the Nishada people, was in love... with a princess he had never even met. Her name was Damayanti. Poets and politicians, servants and princes all praised her to the skies. "She is radiant like the sun," they said. "Full of charm and wit and grace." It was whispered that she had even stirred the hearts of the gods.

With each new description of her beauty, Nala fell more deeply in love. He began to neglect his duties and spend hours dreaming of Damayanti. But until her father, King Bhima, announced that she was ready for marriage, there was nothing for Nala to do but wait.

One day, as Nala sat by the palace lake, a flock of swans landed at the far end of the water. Slowly, they glided up to him. As they drew near, Nala saw their feathers were tinged with gold. He quickly reached out and grabbed the nearest bird by the neck.

The swan opened its beak, and cried out, "O King! Don't kill me! I know that you love Damayanti and I can help. I'll fly to her palace and sing your praises until she loves you too."

Instantly, Nala released his grip on the swan. "Go then," he said, filled with sudden excitement. "Fly to Damayanti, as fast as you can."

The flock of swans took off from the lake. They flew without stopping, until they reached King Bhima's palace, in the city of Vidarbhas. They soared over the palace's high walls, past its closely guarded gates, and spied Princess Damayanti sitting in the pleasure gardens with her maids. Then the swans dropped down amongst them, flapping their wings so their golden feathers shone in the sun.

"What beautiful birds!" cried Damayanti. "Let's catch them!"
The swans scattered and the maids ran after them, while
Damayanti's swan led her down to the lake.

"Princess Damayanti," the swan began.
"Nala, King of the Nishadas, has sent
me to you. He has heard you are
a jewel among women, and
he asks you to be his wife."

Damayanti gasped, but the
swan went on, "Nala is strong,
skilled with horses and with
arrows. He is a hero and a great
general. Never have I seen a man
or god as handsome as Nala..."

"Stop! Stop!" said Damayanti, laughing.
"There's no need to persuade me. Just as Nala has
heard stories about me, so have I heard all about Nala.
You may tell Nala that I am his."

"I will," promised the swan, rising up on his golden wings.

Damayanti lay down in the shady grove. "Nala loves me!"
she whispered to herself, a smile spreading across her face.

But over the next few weeks, Damayanti grew pale and thin.
She pined for Nala. She couldn't eat or sleep, and spent her time
gazing at the sky.

"What's the matter?" asked her father, King Bhima.

"Nothing," Damayanti replied, keeping her love a secret.

The king didn't know what to do. "Is my daughter ill?" he wondered. "If she's sick, why won't she tell me?"

At last, one of Damayanti's maids decided to help. "Damayanti's not ill, Your Highness," she said. "She's in love."

"In love?" repeated the king. He called Damayanti to him at once. "My daughter," he said, "the time has come for you to choose your husband. We must hold a swayamvara ceremony."

The king sent messengers to the far flung corners of his kingdom. "King Bhima announces his daughter's swayamvara!" they trumpeted. "To take place at the palace on the night of the next full moon."

Kings and princes left their palaces in droves, until the kingdom was filled with the sound of elephants, horses and chariots all making their way to Vidarbhas.

Eventually, Nala heard the news, and he too set out. But unknown to Nala, the gods were watching him from the air.

Indra, lord of heaven, Agni, lord of fire, Varuna, lord of water, and Yama, lord of death, had heard the news and all wanted Damayanti for themselves. When they saw Nala's handsome face, they grew anxious.

"He'll win Damayanti for sure," they said. "We need a plan..."

The gods came down from the sky and surrounded Nala on a craggy hilltop near the city.

"Nala, King of the Nishadas, best of kings, will you help us?" they said. "We need you to be a messenger for us!"

"I will," promised Nala. He knew it was dangerous for any man to refuse the gods.

"We four have come down from the sky for Damayanti," said Indra. "Go to Damayanti for us, and tell her we wish to win her. Ask her to choose a husband from among us."

Nala bowed before the gods, but he was angry. "You've no right to send me," he said. "I've set out for Vidarbhas with the same purpose as you. How can I plead your case when I want to win her for myself? Please, ask someone else!"

"It's too late!" said Indra. "You have already promised to help us. You can't go back on your word."

"But I can't enter the palace before the swayamvara," Nala replied. "It's closely-guarded. I'd never get in."

"With the help of the gods," Indra said, "you can do anything."

The next instant, Nala found himself in the palace gardens of Vidarbhas. From behind a pillar, he spied Damayanti, laughing with her friends. Seeing her for the first time, Nala fell more deeply in love than ever. "Her beauty puts the moon's to shame," he thought.

"Who's that man?" asked Damayanti's friends. "He's handsome enough to be a god."

The stranger came forward.

"I am Nala," he said.

Damayanti stretched out her hand to welcome him, but Nala instantly stepped away. "I haven't come here for myself," he said, "but as a messenger of the gods. Indra, Agni, Varuna and Yama ask you to choose one of them as a husband. Now you must decide what to do."

"I am grateful to the gods," said Damayanti, firmly, "but I already know who I'm going to choose for my husband at the swayamvara. I've already sworn that I'm yours."

Nala shook his head. "The gods want to marry you," he said. "How could you want a man instead? I am nothing but dust at their feet. If you marry a god, you'll have the softest silks for clothes, divine garlands to wear around your neck and the most beautiful jewels in the world."

Damayanti's eyes filled with tears. "I praise the gods," she said. "But I still choose you as a husband. Won't you tell me what *you* think I should do?"

"No!" said Nala. "I came with a message from the gods. I can't ask you to do as *I* wish."

Then Damayanti smiled through her tears. "You have delivered the gods' message. Now let me send a message to them," she said.

"Tell the gods to come to my swayamvara. I'll choose you as my husband in their presence. I don't fear the gods, whatever they might say."

"If that's your decision," said Nala, smiling, "I accept it." Then he bowed to Damayanti and returned to the hilltop, where the gods were waiting for him...

"Tell us everything that happened," said the gods. "What did Damayanti say to you?"

So Nala told them. "I did as you asked," he said. "I pleaded your case, but Damayanti's mind was made up. She asks that all four of you come to the place of her swayamvara. She says that in your presence, she'll choose me for a husband."

"We will be there," the gods replied, already rising up to the heavens. "But don't be so sure she'll choose you!"

On the day of the swayamvara, all the love-stricken kings and princes assembled at King Bhima's palace. They were surrounded by their courtiers, all eager to see Damayanti. When the time came, Damayanti entered the hall, dazzling the men with her beauty and stealing their hearts. But Damayanti only had eyes for Nala.

She saw him sitting near the front and walked
up to him... then stopped in shock. For she saw
there wasn't just one Nala, but five.

"The gods are playing a trick on me!" she realized. Damayanti
looked, and looked again, desperately trying to spot the
difference between them. But five identical men stared back at
her, out of five identical pairs of eyes.

The other men stared at Damayanti as she stood transfixed to
the spot. "What is she doing?" they wondered.

Almost without hope, Damayanti prayed to the gods for
mercy. The four gods heard her prayer and were moved. They
finally understood that she truly loved Nala.

In that instant they showed themselves to Damayanti. Then
she saw that four of the men looked at her without blinking.
Their skin was free from dust, their garlands hadn't withered in
the sun and they were floating just above the ground.

"And the fifth man!" Damayanti said to herself. "His garland is beginning to fade. His skin is stained with dust and sweat, and his eyes are blinking in the bright sunlight." Last of all, she saw that the fifth man was the only one with a shadow.

Then Damayanti knew that this man was the true Nala. She picked up a beautiful wreath of flowers and handed it to Nala, as a sign to everyone that she had chosen her husband. Dejected, the other kings and princes left the swayamvara to return to their palaces.

Only the four gods remained. They took on their true forms
and Nala and Damayanti bowed low before them.

"Forgive me for choosing Nala," begged Damayanti.

And because Nala and Damayanti truly loved each other, the
gods forgave them. As wedding gifts, Indra gave Nala the speed
of a god, Agni gave him the power to create fire, Yama the art
of cooking, and Varuna the ability to summon water at will.

King Bhima was overjoyed at his daughter's decision. As the
gods returned to heaven, he began the celebrations for the
wedding of Nala and Damayanti.

The Frog Princess

Once there was a king who had three handsome sons: Alexander, Nicolas and Ivan. He watched them play in their nursery and race around the castle courtyard, and he watched them grow into young men. He waited for the castle to be turned upside down with their weddings... but he waited in vain.

Finally, he summoned all three sons to the throne room. "I've called you here," the king began, "because it's high time you were married. I'm growing old. Soon, I shall be ready to pass on my crown." He paused and looked at each son in turn. "I shall give my crown to the son who finds the most suitable wife."

Nicolas snorted. "Just like that?" he said. "How?"

The king frowned at his middle son's rudeness. "You must climb the tallest tower in the castle and fire an arrow from the top," he told them. "Where it lands, you'll find a wife."

"That's preposterous!" spluttered Nicolas.

The king glared at him. "But you'll do it," he snapped, "or lose your chance to be king."

Nicolas was still grumbling as he stomped up the steps of the tallest tower.

"He's an old man," said Alexander, as he and Nicolas fitted arrows to their bows, "and maybe he's a little crazy. But he *is* the king." Holding his bow high, Alexander faced north, pulled the arrow back and let it fly. With a *twang!* the arrow soared into the air, flew over the moat and sailed on, landing in the grounds of a magnificent manor.

Shrugging, Nicolas turned to face south. Then he too fired his arrow and saw it land on the roof of an ornate townhouse.

Ivan silently put an arrow to his bow. He spun around and let it fly, staring in disbelief as it barely grazed the castle walls before landing in the dark forest. Who could live there?

The three princes raced to the stables where their horses were saddled up, ready to go.

"See you soon," said Alexander, as he leaped onto his horse. "I'll be back with the most beautiful queen at my side."

"And I'll be back with the most dutiful queen beside me," Nicolas grinned.

Ivan simply spurred his horse over the drawbridge and into the forest. Thorny branches tore at his cloak and tree roots threatened to trip his horse, until he was forced to continue on foot. At last, he came to a clearing with a pond, which was covered in lily pads. On the biggest lily pad sat a frog – with Ivan's arrow in her mouth.

Ivan gulped. "There must be a mistake," he said.

The frog opened her mouth and the arrow fell out. "I think you're looking for me," she croaked.

Just then, a fly darted past and the frog caught it with her tongue. Stretching her webbed feet, she jumped from the lily pad and landed with a splat on one of Ivan's muddy boots.

"Looking for you?" repeated Ivan. "Not exactly." He paused. Surely his father hadn't meant him to marry a frog?

"So when's the wedding?" asked the frog, as if she had read his mind.

"Wedding?" cried Ivan, bending down. The frog was covered in pond slime. "I don't think..."

"Weren't you meant to find a wife where your arrow landed?" the frog interrupted, fixing Ivan with her bulging eyes.

"Well, yes," he said.

The frog hopped onto his hand. "Then take me back to the castle as your bride."

"But it's ridiculous," Ivan protested. "Even if you can talk..."

"It's fate," said the frog.

Ivan rode back to the castle with the frog safely in his pocket. "My father won't make me marry a frog," he thought.

Leaving his horse with a castle groom, he darted through a side door, hoping to reach his room before anyone spotted him.

"Let me out," croaked the frog, jumping in his pocket. "I want to see my new home."

Ivan sighed and gently lifted the frog out, his fingers slippery with slime. The frog settled herself on his palm and looked around. "This isn't very grand," she said. "Can't I see the hall?"

Ivan crept to the hall. Inside, servants were rushing around, preparing the wedding feast. "Here," he whispered, holding the frog up so she could see the gaily fluttering banners.

"Ribbit!" she croaked delightedly. With a bound, she jumped onto a long table, hopping over a fruit bowl and a dish of rice. "Oops!" she added, as she collided with a jug.

The jug toppled over and smashed in half, just as the king arrived with Ivan's brothers.

"What's going on?" demanded the king.

"Where's your future wife, Ivan?" chorused Alexander and Nicolas, coming in with their blushing brides-to-be.

"Meet the Lady Anastasia," Alexander announced proudly.

"And Elena, the richest girl in town," added Nicolas.

"Eugh, a frog," squeaked Elena.

The king raised his eyebrows. "Why is there a frog on the table?" he asked.

Ivan quickly went over to the table and put his hand down. The frog hopped onto it. "She's with me," he said, ignoring his brothers' shouts of glee.

"*That's* your bride?" sneered Nicolas.

"Hope Cook has plenty of flies on the menu," said Alexander, laughing at his own joke.

"She found my arrow," Ivan explained, "but I don't have to marry her." He turned to his father. "Do I?"

"That was the arrangement," said the king firmly. "The weddings will take place in the chapel immediately."

"It's between us then!" Nicolas said triumphantly to Alexander, as the brothers left the chapel with their brides.

"Wait," the king put in. "Now you're married, I want to set all three, ahem, brides, some tests."

The first test was to sew the king a shirt by morning. Ivan picked up his frog-wife and fled to his room in despair.

"Don't worry, Ivan," the frog said soothingly. "Just go to bed."

The minute Ivan was asleep, the frog transformed herself into a radiant princess. She clapped her hands and a mound of the finest linen appeared. Shaking it out, she began to sew.

When Ivan showed his father the shirt next morning, the king was delighted. "The shirts of your brothers' brides are dishcloths," he declared, "but this is a shirt fit for a banquet. Can your frog bake too? Tomorrow, I want three loaves."

"She's no frog. She's a sorceress in disguise," Anastasia muttered to Elena. "Let's spy on her as she makes her bread."

But the frog was too clever for them. While they watched, she took a lump of dough and threw it on the fire. The moment they left for their rooms, she became a princess again. With fresh dough, she began to bake the lightest, sweetest loaf.

The king was disgusted by the charred dough offered by Anastasia and Elena, but the frog's golden loaf delighted him. "Ivan's frog has won him the crown," he declared. "I'll hold a ball this evening to congratulate Ivan and his frog princess."

As Ivan entered the hall that night, he heard the courtiers whispering about him. But their jeers turned to gasps of amazement as a dazzling woman came in, wearing a billowing ball gown and a crown encrusted with jewels.

"The Princess Vasilisa," announced an usher.

Vasilisa turned to Ivan with a smile. "Hello husband," she murmured.

Ivan stared in astonishment. Was this vision his wife?

"Let the feast begin!" cried the king, raising his goblet.

Anastasia scowled. "What's that frog up to now?" she hissed to Elena. "Let's keep an eye on her."

During the meal, Anastasia saw Vasilisa pouring water from her glass into her right sleeve. Clumsily, she copied her. Then Elena spotted Vasilisa tucking chicken bones up her left sleeve and did the same.

As Ivan led Vasilisa onto the dance floor, she waved her right arm and a shining lake appeared. Anastasia waved hers and splashed the king. Princess Vasilisa twirled around... and seven snow-white swans flew from her left sleeve. A ripple of applause went around the room.

Jealous, Elena swept her arm in a wide arc – and hit several guests with greasy chicken bones. Alexander and Nicolas took their wives and left the ball early.

So did Ivan. He had fallen in love with his frog princess. Hurrying back to their room, he found her frog skin and threw it on the fire.

"Ivan, no!" cried Vasilisa, when she saw what he'd done. "I was under a curse," she told him, "forced to be a frog by day and only human at night. But it would have lasted for just three more days and then I could have ruled beside you." As she spoke, she began to fade. "Now I belong to Koshchei the Deathless," she said faintly, "and we can never be together. Goodbye Ivan." Ivan leaped up to take her in his arms and found himself clutching empty air.

He left the castle that same evening, vowing he would only return when he'd found his wife. Ivan asked everyone he met about Koshchei, but no one could help. He crossed dark forests and swift-flowing rivers, climbed mountains and trekked through valleys until, finally, he was stopped by an old man.

"I know all about you, prince," said the man, before Ivan could say a word. "You seek Princess Vasilisa. Here," he added, handing Ivan a ball of wool. "Follow this. It will take you to her."

"Thank you," cried Ivan, rolling the wool along the ground.

The ball of wool rolled down a rocky path to a bear. Ivan quickly loaded his bow but as he took aim the bear begged for mercy. "Spare me and I'll help you one day," growled the bear. Taking pity on him, Ivan agreed.

A little while later, a drake flew overhead. As Ivan grabbed his bow, the bird swooped down before him. "Spare me and I shall help you," promised the drake. Once again, Ivan agreed. The wool wound on and Ivan followed it to the sea. There, stranded on the shore, was a pike. "Please, throw me back," the pike gasped, "and I'll help you one day." Ivan scooped up the fish and put it back in the sea.

At last, the wool came to rest in front of an old woman, at the edge of a forest. "I've come to rescue my wife from Koshchei the Deathless," Ivan told her. "Can you help?" The old woman sucked her toothless gums. "It won't be easy," she said. "You'll have to destroy his soul and that's trapped in a needle. The needle is caught in the yolk of an egg and the egg is inside a duck."

"The duck is locked in a chest which rests on the top of this tree," she went on, pointing to a vast oak tree.

Ivan looked at the tree towering above him. There was no way he could reach the chest. As he despaired, the bear he had met came lumbering up. Silently, the bear gripped the tree and shook it. The chest fell to the ground, broke open and a duck flew out. In seconds, it was caught by the drake Ivan had spared. But as he watched, the duck laid its egg, which plummeted into the sea.

"No!" Ivan shouted, racing to the shore.

The pike Ivan had saved heard his cries. Diving under the waves, he found the egg and brought it to Ivan. With trembling hands, Ivan cracked the egg open. Inside was a needle, just as the old woman had said. Ivan fished it out, wiped it on his tunic and snapped it in two.

A crash of thunder shook the forest and there was Princess Vasilisa, standing before him. "Ivan, you saved me," she cried, her dark eyes shining with joy.

"Let's go home."